For th*E* wind
—*PG*

For Mirna

the wish
for you
a miracle

—*Elle and Erik*

Copyright © 2006 by Lemniscaat b.v. Rotterdam
Originally published in the Netherlands under the title *De Wens* by Lemniscaat b.v. Rotterdam
All rights reserved—CIP data is available
Printed and bound in Belgium
First U.S. edition

FRONT STREET
An Imprint of Boyds Mills Press, Inc.
A Highlights Company

815 Church Street
Honesdale, Pennsylvania 18431

The Wish

Elle **van Lieshout** & Erik **van Os**

Paula **Gerritsen**

FRONT STREET 8 LEMNISCAAT

JUL 0 9 2007

Far away from the rest of the world
lived a woman named Lila. She had a
small house on a cliff, overlooking the
sea. Year after year she plowed the fields
and planted seeds.

In spring she sowed sunflowers.

In summer she picked beans.

In autumn she collected apples for applesauce.

In winter she sat by
the fire most of the time.

During the long, cold winter, Lila
thought spring would never come.
The vegetable garden was
barren and frozen. There were
no flowers, no beans. Lila was
finishing the last of the applesauce,
and she was hungry.

Then one cold night, when Lila
looked up through the window
into the dark sky, a star fell.
Thank goodness.

Lila made a wish.

The next morning, Lila found a
bag of flour in front of the house.

Happily, she baked the best
bread she had ever baked.

The bread lasted a week. When
the last crumb was gone, Lila
was hungry again.

Another star fell.

The next day, Lila found another
bag of flour in front of her door.
Every time the bread was gone,
another star fell.

That's how she survived the
long, cold winter.

Of course, she could have wished
for something completely different
from a bag of flour.

A table filled with delicious food and drinks, for example ...

or fancy clothes ...

or a mountain of gold and diamonds,
a carriage, and a palace with servants.

Most people would wish for
something fancy when a star falls.
But not Lila. It didn't even cross her mind ...

except on the night before her birthday.
That night, she wished for two cakes ...

and a tractor—
shiny red—

with a chauffeur.